# NO SAX
# PLEASE, WE'RE
# EGYPTIAN

Adapted by Maureen Spurgeon from
original Cosgrove Hall Productions
script by Brian Trueman
and directed by Chris Randall.

CARNIVAL

Carnival
An imprint of the Children's Division
of the Collins Publishing Group
8 Grafton Street, London W1X 3LA

Published by Carnival 1988

Reprinted 1989

Count Duckula is a registered trademark of
THAMES TELEVISION plc.
Copyright © COSGROVE HALL PRODUCTIONS 1987

ISBN 0 00 194473 8

Printed & bound in Great Britain by
PURNELL BOOK PRODUCTION LIMITED
A MEMBER OF BPCC plc

There are very few brave enough to venture far enough into the Transylvanian Alps to feel the cold fingers of fear creeping through the grey mists, swirling shadows of terror and foreboding . . .

And at the very heart stands Castle Duckula, ancestral home of a long line of the most evil vampire barons, a place where, even today, dread voices may be heard, echoing strangely . . .

"It's Nanny, Master Duckula, with your hot cocoa and choccy biccies!"

Just the thing for a hungry vampire duck, Count Duckula decided. "Come in, Nanny!" he called.

His manservant, Igor, immediately covered his eyes and gave a massive shudder. Count Duckula covered his ears.

The resounding crash came as expected – but it still made them jump out of their skins, bits of brick and stone flew all around.

"Nanny . . ." groaned Duckula, reeling back from the hole in the wall. "*Why* can't you come in through the door?"

"The door!" gasped Nanny, clutching her forehead with one podgy hand. "I forgot about that!"

"I give up!" wailed Duckula. "I give up!"

"Cocoa and choccy biccies!" announced Nanny in reply. "There!"

Down crashed the tray on the table – and up went all the cutlery high into the air, thudding into Duckula's chair and framing his head just like the star in a knife-throwing act!

"I'm not standing any more of this!" Duckula snarled through a gritted beak. "I'm giving up my title!"

"Oh, Sir!" said Igor, deeply shocked. "Come with me to the Picture Gallery! Let me remind you of your proud inheritance!"

Count Duckula followed somewhat unwillingly. Little did he realise how much interest there was in Castle Duckula that particular day . . .

"I likes the look of that there castle," growled a gruff voice, and a crowd of sinister black figures suddenly appeared. "Castle Duckula, ain't it, Burt?"

"That's right, Chief!" nodded Burt. "High quality dungeons, good assortment of antique prisoners, big collection of family portraits! That's what our Burglars' Guide says!"

"Valuable paintings, eh?" mused Ruffles. "Okay, you lot! Get the gear out!"

Meanwhile, Igor and Duckula were touring the gallery, Igor was quite enjoying the sense of occasion.

"And this, Milord," he droned on, pointing a bony finger, "is Count Duckula the Third. A delightful portrait of His Grace at an early age, biting the neck of his teddy bear!"

"Yeah?" yawned Duckula, trying to keep his thick eyelids from drooping any further.

"Why, I remember, Milord, when your great, great, great grandfather . . ."

But even as he spoke, Ruffles' gang were already scaling the castle walls . . .

"Come on, lads!" urged Ruffles. "Another fifty feet, and we're there!"

Next minute, he had faltered to a stop, as the most terrible sound reached his ears.

"Makes your flesh creep, don't it?" he shuddered. "Wonder if it's a werewolf?"

But it was only Nanny singing to herself as she whirled around with her feather duster. Trouble only began when she decided to shake it out of the window . . .

"Ah . . . Ah . . ." Ruffles could feel a big sneeze coming on. "Choo!"

Too bad they were all roped together. Because, as Ruffles fell to the ground, so did all the rest, with their loud cries of "Aaaagh! Aaaaagh!" even being heard in the Picture Gallery – where Igor was still trying to educate Count Duckula.

"Then we come, Sir, to your great uncle's great uncle, the Archduck Merganser, the famous Egyptologist who spent a lifetime searching the Great Pyramid, a storehouse of buried treasure!"

Ruffles started to listen carefully . . . It seemed as if scaling up the walls of Castle Duckula for a second time would be well worth the trouble . . .

"You see that pyramid in the painting, Milord? The Archduck had ventured inside to explore the secret depths of the Pharoah Upshi's tomb, when there entered two extremely strange figures." Igor paused dramatically. "It was Hoomite, High Priest of the sun god Ra, and his assistant, Yubi!"

"Go on, Igor!" Duckula urged him, now completely enthralled. "What happened next?"

"Everything went black, Sir. And the Archduck knew no more."

"Knew no more what?"

"Knew no more than I do where the mystic saxophone lay hidden!"

"Mystic saxophone?" echoed Duckula blankly.

"What the Archduck was searching for, Milord! I'm sure I mentioned it . . ."

"You did not!" Duckula was most indignant.

"That's right!" burst out Ruffles, hanging from the window sill. "He never mentioned it!"

"I apologise, Sir," said Igor with a bow. "Milord, it's rather stuffy in here. Excuse me while I open a window . . ."

"Aaaaagh!" screamed Ruffles – which was just about the only thing anyone can say when being knocked from a window sill!

"Aaaagh!" screamed the gang, wishing once more that they were not all tied together, and falling below with a succession of dull thuds.

"What's that, Igor?" enquired Duckula. "Sounds like falling bodies hitting the deck!"

"That will be Nanny making the pastry, Milord. Shall I continue?"

"What, about the mystic saxophone? Yeah, that does sound more interesting!"

"Well, Sir," said Igor. "Legend has it that anyone who plays it has the greatest power in the world!"

"Wow!" breathed Duckula. "I could be famous! I could fill the Hollywood Bowl! Madison Square Gardens! Transylvania Roxy!"

Igor chuckled to himself. This was a chance to straighten Duckula out – he knew that the dark powers of the mystic saxophone would lead him not to stardom, but a life of evil. He would be saved at last!

"Get ready, Igor!" he shouted, rushing down to the crypt, ready to leap into his favourite coffin which would start Castle Duckula travelling high above the Transylvanian Alps. "We're off to Egypt, Valley of the Kings!"

The streaks of yellow and red flashes made Ruffles and his gang shiver and tremble, as they prepared to scale the Castle walls yet again, clutching hard at its cold, stone surface as it leapt high into the air.

"W-what's happening?" gasped Ruffles.

"Oh . . ." Burt moaned. "I – I don't like this . . ."

But they could do nothing, except hold on – until Castle Duckula shuddered and jolted to a halt amid the giant pyramids!

"We're here!" announced Count Duckula. "Outside, everyone!"

"And if you've broken any of the best china, Master Duckula," said Nanny, "you'll go straight to your room!"

"Nanny! Be silent!" scolded Igor. "Come!"

They began making their way out of the front door of Castle Duckula and across the sand towards the giant pyramid – little knowing they were being watched at every step . . .

"Funny looking mountains, ain't they, Chief?" commented Burt.

"They're pyramids!" snorted Ruffles. "Ha-ha! That daft duck has given us a free trip to Egypt!" He laughed again. "Come on lads! We'll get that mystic saxophone before they do – just as soon as we find a window!"

This last remark was overheard by the bats living inside the cuckoo clock which timed Castle Duckula on its travels. And they never could resist a chance to amuse themselves.

"Hey, Sviatoslav!" said one.

"Ya, Dimitri?"

"Vat are zey callink a pyramid wiz windows?"

"How should I know vat they are calling a pyramid wiz windows?"

"A tomb wiz a view! Ha-ha-ha!"

Sviatoslav was feeling a bit dim that morning. "So vere is zis pyramid wiz windows?"

"Oh, flap off, you silly old bat!" said Dimitri, and they both went inside the clock again . . . just as Ruffles and Burt had decided that it might be best to use the pyramid door!

"Now, you lot," Ruffles snarled, looking much the worse for wear, "we're gonna set a trap for this Count Duckula, okay? So . . ."

But nobody heard what he said next. With a loud wail, he disappeared down a hole, a rope tying him and his gang together, as usual, and pulling them down with him – just as one of the gang was about to grab a handful of jewels from the nearest treasure chest!

"What was that?" asked Duckula, feeling the ground shake beneath his webbed feet. "All those bangs and crashes!"

"Well, sir," Igor responded after some thought, "it can't be Nanny's pastry this time!"

A little more First Aid, and a few more bandages –
and Ruffles' gang were ready to go into action yet
again . . . this time, in one of the long chambers inside
the pyramid, where a huge slab hung high up, tied by
a rope in the middle of the room . . .

"So," snarled Ruffles, "when that Count Duckula
and his lot comes through the door – here! Pay
attention, Burt!"

"I am paying attention!" Burt snapped back,
sounding a bit muffled because of all the bandages.

"That's a mummy you're talking to, you idiot! I'm
over here!"

"Eh?" Burt blinked once or twice. "Oh, yus . . .
Yus, Chief. Sorry . . ."

"Now," continued Ruffles, with an air of long-suffering patience, "what happens is this. They comes in through the door, trips over the rope, then down comes the slab with a wallop – and the mystic saxophone is mine!"

"That's clever!" Burt had to admit, looking from one end of the chamber to the other. "But, which door?"

"Don't make no difference . . ." Ruffles began to explain, then put a bandaged finger to his lips. "Sssh . . . Hear them coming? Time for some action!"

In a flash, Ruffles and Burt were either side of the door, with the rest of the gang and pressing themselves flat against the wall.

"No, no, Nanny!" came Duckula's voice. "I'm telling you, this is the door!"

"Are you sure, Duckyboos?" Nanny wavered. "I think this is the door!"

And, accompanied by the usual chorus of bangs and crashes, Nanny walked right through the wall, flattening most of the gang. Ruffles and Burt could only stand and gape in stunned amazement as she led Igor and Count Duckula across the chamber and out through the other side – with a lot more smashes and bashes.

"There you are!" she exclaimed triumphantly. "I told you this was the way!"

"I-I don't believe it . . ." stammered Ruffles, once the dust had settled. "I-I just don't believe it!"

Suddenly they heard Duckula's voice once more.

"I'm just going back, Nanny! Something I saw . . . !"

"Right!" grinned Ruffles. "*Now* we'll nab him!"

They all held their breath as Duckula edged into the room.

"Here we are," he muttered to himself, reaching out towards the rope and tugging hard. "This could be useful!"

The rope broke. Out went Duckula, dragging his piece behind him. And, down came the slab, flattening Ruffles and Burt!

More bandages, splints and crutches later, Ruffles and Burt were still planning to beat Duckula – this time, with a giant catapult trap!

"Elastic bands stretched across the corridor?" growled Ruffles. "Right! Now . . . we pushes this rock till the band's at full stretch, okay?"

"Okay!" answered the gang.

"Then, once the rock's in place," went on Ruffles, "we puts this 'ere peg in the ground to keep the rock steady!"

"Okay!" came the chorus again.

"Then," continued Ruffles, "when that flipping Count Duckula and his crew comes along, we pulls the peg out, and wallop! They've had it! All together, then – push!"

"U-r-r-rgh!" Ruffles, Burt and the gang groaned together, pushing back the rock against the stretch of the elastic bands. "Oof! U-r-r-rgh!"

"Right!" puffed Ruffles, as soon as the rock was in place. "Drop the peg in the hole!"

"Peg?" echoed Burt. "I thought you had the peg!"

"I gave it to you!" cried Ruffles, with a sense of mounting desperation.

"It's back there, where we started!" shouted one of the gang, trying to be helpful. "I'll get it!"

Without thinking, he dashed back. But, that rock was a whole lot faster!

"Whoa-ow-ow---!" The cry resounded through the pyramid, as it catapulted them along – right through to the outside!

Meanwhile, inside, Igor was just about finishing his investigations.

"From what it said in the Archduck Merganser's diary, Sir, I think we must be nearing the ancient relic . . ."

"We never got away from her!" grinned Duckula, glancing around at Nanny and chuckling at his own joke.

"No, not Nanny!" snapped Igor, quite ignoring Duckula's wit. "The mystic saxophone! And from now on, we should all look out for traps!"

"Traps?" repeated Duckula.

"Traps meant to stop anyone from reaching the saxophone, Milord . . ."

"Don't talk such rubbish, Igor!" scoffed Duckula, stamping his foot with impatience. "There aren't any . . . Aaaaagh . . .!"

Next thing Count Duckula knew, he was falling down a deep shaft, landing with such a bump that stars whirled his eyes, and everything went black . . .

Then, a strange-sounding voice broke the silence.

"He is coming round!"

"Oh . . .!" Duckula mumbled feebly. "Wh-where am I?"

"Your are in the temple of the great god, Ra!" boomed the voice. "You, who have trespassed on Pharoah Upshi's sacred tomb!"

"Oh, no . . ." gasped Duckula. He tried sitting up, but found that his ankles were being held down by metal bands. "Wh-ho are you?"

"I am Hoomite," came the answer, "High Priest of the Great God, Ra! And this is my assistant, Yubi!"

"Delighted, I'm sure!" gushed Yubi. It was clear he meant to be friendly. "Who might you be?"

"Yes," said Duckula wearily. "You just told me!"

"No!" yelled Hoomite. "Who might you be?"

"I know!" Duckula yelled back. "You said so already!"

"Yubi!" Hoomite yelled again. "You try!"

"Listen, I am Yubi! Right?"

"Wrong! I am – you are!" said Duckula.

"There, master!" Yubi cried. "He is Yewar!"

"I am not!" Duckula shouted at the top of his voice. "I am not!"

"Ah . . ." Hoomite nodded wisely. "So you are, Nott. He is not Yewar, he is Nott!"

"Oo-o-o-oooh!" screamed Duckula. "I can't stand any more!"

"Of course, you can't stand any more!" agreed Yubi. "We have tied you to the sacrificial altar!"

"And all who trespass in Pharoah Upshi's tomb shall die!" ended Hoomite. "Legend says that when the god Ra has had enough human sacrifice, Upshi shall rise from the dead!"

"H-human sacrifice?" gulped Duckula. "You can't do this to me!"

"Well, more or less sacrifice – give or take a feather!" insisted Hoomite. "In order that the great Upshi may rule again. Yes – he shall have human sacrifice!"

Duckula answered without thinking: "Who, Ra?"

"And Upshi rises!" ended Hoomite – which, of course, was the signal for Duckula to forget his bonds, jump down from the altar and lead the singing:

"Hoorah, and up she rises! Hoorah, and up she rises, Hoorah, and up she rises, ear-ly in the morning!"

"Put him in the long boat with a hose-pipe on him!" they all sang together. "Put him in the long boat with a hose-pipe on him! Put him in the long boat with a hose-pipe on him . . ."

"Excuse me . . ." Yubi gulped suddenly. "I-I think I'm going to be seasick!" And, hand over his mouth, he rushed towards the nearest wall, pressing a knob almost by accident.

Nobody was more surprised than Duckula when part of the wall slid back . . .

"Nanny!" he cried.

"Ooooh!" gasped Nanny. "Now, then . . ."

There was a long silence, whilst Hoomite and Yubi stared hard.

"It is Upshi!" whispered Hoomite in awe. "He has cast off his wrappings!"

"Here!" Nanny burst out. "Watch it, saucy!"

"Upshi?" repeated Duckula, in some surprise.

"Yes . . ." whispered Yubi, and pointed to a picture painted on the wall of the pyramid. "Look at that! Look!"

So, Duckula looked, his eyes growing wider and wider.

"I – I don't believe it!" he murmured at last. "The only thing more like Nanny is – Nanny!"

Hoomite and Yubi had already fallen to the ground in front of her.

"Upshi rises! Upshi rises!"

"Now, don't talk so silly!" Nanny scolded, looking down in the general direction of her feet. "Who might you be?"

"He knows us!" Hoomite cried out in delight. "He knows us!"

"I see . . ." said Nanny. "He, Nosus. But, who might you be?"

"Oh, no!" groaned Duckula. "I'm not going through all that again!"

"Come along, Nanny!" he cried, picking her up before she could say anything else. "We're going!"

"Follow them!" commanded Ruffles, pointing a bandaged finger along the corridor.

But Duckula, Nanny and Igor had already reached the treasure house, staring all around in wonder.

"Oh, look at that!" breathed Nanny, her beady little eyes on a bandaged figure in the middle of the room. "Poor soul! I expect he fell off his camel!"

"Nanny!" exclaimed Duckula. "That's a mummy!"

"Silly me!" Nanny giggled. "I expect she fell off her camel!"

"Oooh! Duckyboos!" she went on, before anyone could draw breath to reply. "Isn't that a nice vase? It would look lovely in the lobby!"

"Nanny . . . please don't . . ." begged Duckula, waving his hands at her. "You'll drop it!"

"I'll do what, Master Duckula?"

"Drop it!"

"Oh . . ." Nanny blinked a few times, then opened her flabby hands. "Very good, Milord!"

"Look at that!" wailed Duckula, eyeing the shattered pieces. "The priceless converted to the worthless . . ."

"By the brainless!" finished Igor. But, Duckula was not really listening . . .

"Hey, wait a minute! Do you see what I see, among all those bits of vase? It's the Mystic Saxophone!"

"One single blow, Nanny," murmured Igor in a tone of deep satisfaction, "and we shall be the servants of the Emperor of Evil!"

"Oooh!" squealed Nanny, putting her hands over her ears. "What a noise! It's enough to waken the dead!"

Igor only smiled to himself, rubbing his thin hands together to see mummies beginning to come to life. But that smile seemed to freeze in horror when they started dancing to the accompaniment of the flashing lights of hieroglyphics on the wall!

He could not resist raising it to his lips, and giving a few blasts to hear what it would sound like!

"Oh, no!" he groaned, looking all around in horror. "Wh-what is happening?"

"'Ere!" Ruffles burst out. "Seems there's a party going on! After you, lads!"

"Come along Mister Igor!" cried Nanny, obviously loving every minute. "Everyone's joining in the fun!"

"Upshi rises!" cried Hoomite and Yubi, rushing into the chamber. "Upshi rises!"

"Nanny!" Igor shouted above the din. "I believe these gentlemen are requesting the next dance! Aaaagh . . .!"

But with all the noise which was going on, Hoomite and Yubi hardly heard his cries of pain as they rushed towards Nanny, bowing down in worship. Nanny was delighted!

Everyone agreed that the party was a great success
– especially with Duckula playing the saxophone for
all he was worth! Only Igor seemed at all
disapproving, fingering his wrist-watch every so often
and glancing anxiously in the direction of his master.

"Milord," he broke in at last, "I don't want to spoil
the party – but I think you ought to know it is nearly
time for us to return to Transylvania!"

"Oh, don't be so boring Mr Igor!" Nanny spoke up,
between a few puffs and blows. "You always worry too
much!"

But already, the cuckoo clock had begun to whir,
making the first rumbles of movement echo
throughout Castle Duckula.

Then, lighting up the Egyptian sky with bright red and yellow flashes, it began lifting up from the sands, leaving Pharoah Upshi's pyramid, Nanny's party – and Count Duckula – behind . . .

And only when the final note of music had faded did Duckula realise that he had missed the last castle home.

"I did tell you it was time, Milord!" Igor reminded him reproachfully.

"All right, all right!" snapped Duckula, already tired of helping to hold up a placard reading TRANSYLVANIA with one hand, and trying to thumb a lift with the other. "Nobody likes a know-all!"

And, just then, two camels carrying a few mummies, Ruffles, Burt and the gang plodded their way past . . ."